HISTORY OF ROCK AND ROLL

The Roots of Rock
Volume I
Pre-1950's

Written by: Stuart Kallen
Edited by: Robert Italia

Published by Abdo & Daughters, 6537 Cecilia Circle, Bloomington, Minnesota 55435

Library bound edition distributed by Rockbottom Books, Pentagon Tower, P.O. Box 36036, Minneapolis, Minnesota 55435

Copyright© 1989 by Abdo Consulting Group, Inc., Pentagon Tower, P.O. Box 36036, Minneapolis, Minnesota 55435. International copyrights reserved in all countries. No part of this book may be reproduced in any form without written permission from the publisher. Printed in the United States.

Library of Congress Number: 89-084914   ISBN: 0-939179-72-5

Cover Photos by: Michael Ochs Archive
Illustrations by: Michael Ochs Archive

LIBRARY
HOLBEIN SCH.
MT. HOLLY, NJ

INTRODUCTION

Every time we tune our radios or T.V.s to a Rock-n-Roll channel, we are listening to history. By listening to the music of everyone from Bob Dylan to XTC, we can hear the influence of someone like Woody Guthrie or Muddy Waters who in turn was influenced by the many unknown folk musicians who came before them. Many rock stars of today, in order to improve their own musicianship and songwriting abilities, spend their time listening to, and studying the lives of, the great musicians who went before them. In this book we are going to look into the lives of the great musicians who have left their mark on popular music in the past, and will leave their mark well into the future.

ONCE UPON A TIME IN AMERICA

With her wide open spaces and abundance of natural resources, the United States is known as a "melting pot" of humanity. During the late 1800's, wave after wave of cultures came to America to start life anew and to exchange ideas with the people who had come before them. With them they brought their music.

THE PIANO'S IN THE MAIL

At the begining of this century, the U.S. Mail Service opened up a whole new world to people who lived in rural areas. Huge mail order houses like Sears and Robuck shipped violins, guitars and banjos anywhere in the United States. In 1901 a person could order a piano from a catalogue for $98! These instruments found their way into the hands of people in the most remote regions of the country, and they adapted their traditional music to fit whatever instrument was available.

Around the turn of the century, these newly aquired guitars and pianos helped give birth to a new musical style known as the Blues. Many poor people in rural areas had a very hard life. They sang about their hardships (and joys) in a song pattern that would repeat one verse twice and then follow with a different verse. For example: "Woke up this morning with the blues all 'round my head / Woke up this morning with the blues all 'round my head / It's the worst feeling that I ever had." Guitars, too, were being played differently. Sometimes the guitar was played with a pen knife or a bottleneck, a style known as "slide guitar." The Blues started out on the farms and in the fields of rural plantations. But soon entertainers were introducing the Blues to white audiences in minstrel shows and steamboats.

AND ALL THAT JAZZ

While people like W.C. Handy were introducing white audiences to the blues in Memphis, another kind of music was being introduced in New Orleans. A cornet player named Buddy Bolden thought of playing a melody louder than the rest of the band, making up the tune as he went along, playing whatever notes fit. Buddy Bolden spent most of his life in mental institutions and never recorded, but in 1902, a new musical form called Jazz was invented by him. Jazz and its cousin Swing became all the rage in America. In fact the 1920's are known by many as "The Jazz Age."

TIN PAN ALLEY

Most of the popular music in the 20's came out of Tin Pan Alley in New York City where professional songwriters worked. Tin Pan Alley got its name because the noise from the many run down pianos all playing at once sounded like a tin works! Classically trained musicians such as Irving Berlin and the Gershwin Brothers wrote many of the classics that have been redone by numerous entertainers in the last half century.

QUICK SPINS

Popular music was given a big boost by the invention of the flat record that played at 78 revolutions per minute. Before this invention, records were wax cylinders that were very fragile. The phonograph record caught on quickly and was sold to people at "phonograph parlors" where people would listen to records through headphones.

HILLBILLY MUSIC

Two men, one from Texas and the other from Virginia, would unknowingly change the music business forever. "Eck" Robertson and Henry Gilliland showed up at the offices of Victor Records in New York City in 1922. One man was dressed as a cowboy the other as a Confederate general from the Civil War. The men demanded that they be recorded. Just to get rid of them, somebody at Victor recorded them playing "Arkansas Traveler" and "Sally Gooden" on violins. Although the playing style was incredibly primitive, the record was released, and it sold enough for Victor to send talent scouts to the South looking for other "Hillbilly Music" to record.

SING THE BLUES

On February 14, 1920, a black woman named Mamie Smith made the first blues record. "Crazy Blues" sold so well that soon all the record companies were getting into the Blues market. The talent scouts who were down South looking for hillbillies to record soon got the call to look for Blues artists as well. These new, hot selling records were called "race records." The term "race record" was used until 1949 to describe most music done by black people. Then the music industry magazine "Billboard" began using the term Rhythm and Blues or R & B to describe the same music.

THE BIRTH OF ROCK-N-ROLL

When the record companies began sending talent scouts down South and recording whatever music they found there, they started introducing people from one region of the country to music from other regions. Thus, the Blues of the Mississippi Delta were being heard in Texas, and the hillbilly songs of North Carolina were being heard in Memphis. But most importantly, all these original styles and players were being heard by people everywhere because of the invention of radio. The blending in of all these different styles created a whole new sound: Rock-n-Roll!

WOODY GUTHRIE — THE GRANDADDY OF FOLK MUSIC

During the Great Depression in America many people were put out of work. The suffering was made even worse by a severe drought that lasted for many years, drying up the farm soil and turning it into raging dust storms. The southern part of the U.S. became known as the "Dust Bowl." Thousands of people were forced to

Woody Guthrie, America's Folk hero.

abandon their farms. With nowhere to go many people headed to California where they hoped they could find work harvesting fruits and vegetables. Woody Guthrie, the man who inspired Bob Dylan, was one of the "Dust Bowl Refugees." Woody sang about the hard lives of the people he met on the road - people hopping freight trains and driving rickety, old Model T Fords across the American desert, looking for the "Garden of Eden" that was California in the 1930's.

Woodrow Wilson Guthrie was born July 14, 1912 in Okemah, Oklahoma. Okemah was an oil town where men came from all over to work the oil rigs. The population of Okemah was about $1/3$ black, $1/3$ white, $1/3$ Indian. Woody Guthrie got his first musical experience playing in the many saloons that filled up with workers wanting to relax after a hard day in the oil fields.

JUST A RAMBLIN' HOBO

When Woody Guthrie was a young man the Great Depression hit Oklahoma. Suddenly left without a home, Woody began riding the rails and staying in hobo camps with the homeless families of America. It was there that Guthrie began making up songs about what was happening all around him. While some of Woody's songs were sad, most had a sense of humor, poking fun at people who gave the poor travelers a hard time and singing about the problems of common folk in funny ways. Woody said he never wanted to write sad songs to make people feel bad when he could write songs to make them smile.

Woody Guthrie's most famous song is "This Land Is Your Land." The song sums up Woody's outlook on life. "This land is your land/ This land is my land/ From California/ To the New York island/ From the redwood forest/ To the Gulf stream waters./ This land was made for you and me." The song is so well loved that there has even been talk over the years of making "This Land Is Your Land" the national anthem!

Woody spent much of his time helping workers get better pay and working conditions. Guthrie also played benefits for the needy and wrote articles for newspapers calling attention to the homeless people who were desperate for food and jobs.

THE DEATH OF WOODY GUTHRIE

Before Woody became nationally famous, he was stricken with Huntington's Chorea, a disease that paralyzes the mind and the body. While he was wasting away in a sanitarium in New Jersey, the Weavers, a folk group made up of Woody's friends, had a number one hit with "This Land Is Your Land." Woody's mind and body were too paralyzed by the disease at this point for him to even understand his success. However, young Bob Dylan had been visiting him in the hospital and had learned all his songs. Dylan says his success in the early 60's is a direct result of Woody's inspiration. Dylan even imitated Guthrie's looks on his album covers!

Woody's son Arlo Guthrie had a big hit in the 60's with "Alice's Restaurant" and in the 70's with "City of New Orleans." Arlo continues to record

Woody Guthrie.

and tour in the 80's. Arlo, too, is involved in many worthwhile causes, from cleaning up the Hudson River to feeding the poor.

Woody Guthrie has been a huge influence on generations of music makers and folk singers. His example of helping poor people and fighting injustice has inspired many people. As Woody sang, "This land was made for you and me."

ROOSEVELT SYKES — THE HONEYDRIPPER

Back in the 1930's most of the lumber used to build America came from the South. Almost all of the laborers in the logging, sawmill and turpentine camps were black men. Many of the great Bluesmen travelled around to the camps playing for the tired workers. They had to be good because these rugged laborers were a tough audience. Roosevelt Sykes was one of the great piano players who toured the camps of southern Mississippi and later the honky-tonks of East St. Louis and Chicago.

THE RUNAWAY

Roosevelt Sykes was born January 31, 1906 in Helena, Arkansas. When he was fifteen he ran away from home to get away from the hard work on his grandfather's farm. To hear Sykes tell it, "I'm leaving here. There must be something better somewhere. I can't do no worser."

Sykes rode the rails and highways playing music wherever he went. To earn extra money, Sykes bootlegged whiskey, operated a cab and ran barbecue joints. But music was always Roosevelt's main focus. Over the course of his fifty year career, Sykes (known professionally as "The Honeydripper" because he sang so sweetly) played with most of the great Blues musicians of the century.

The Honeydripper's recording career began in 1929, and Sykes released one record every month from 1934 until 1942! Sykes inspired greats like Muddy Waters and Memphis Slim along with thousands of white record buyers who loved his great songs such as "The Honeydripper" and "Nighttime's the Right Time."

ROBERT JOHNSON — THEY SAY HE SOLD HIS SOUL TO THE DEVIL

If ever a man existed who was the essence of legend, it was Robert Johnson. Murdered at the age of 24 or 25, Johnson's life story is a tale of talent, tragedy and myth — the story of a talented man consumed by a passion for life, love, and music.

Although Johnson's music formed the bedrock on which Blues and Rock-n-Roll were built, little was known about his early years. Best guesses place his birthdate at sometime in 1914, in Robinsonville, Mississippi.

PLAY MAGIC FINGERS

When Johnson was just a young boy he taught himself to play guitar and to play it with lightning speed! People flocked around Robert to watch his fingers because they couldn't believe their ears. The travel bug bit him when he was a young man. Robert rambled and played in Arkansas, Louisiana, St. Louis, Memphis and Dallas.

THE DEVIL MADE ME DO IT!

Johnson's relatives said in later years that Robert sold his soul to the devil to become a great guitarist, and they could even name the country crossroads where the deal was made. People believed this rumor when they heard Johnson's superhuman guitar playing. Blues researchers say that Johnson once met a man named Ike Zinneman, who was born in Alabama but lived in the Mississippi Delta. Ike told Robert that he learned to play guitar by visiting graveyards at midnight. Nothing is known about Zinneman, so it is impossible to know how he might have influenced Johnson.

The fact that Johnson felt he was chased by demons is revealed in the songs "Me and the Devil Blues" and "Hellhound on My Trail." The lyrics to one of his songs sum up how Johnson felt:

> "You may bury my body, ooh down by the side/ So my old evil spirit can get on a Greyhound Bus and ride."

JOHNSON'S BIG BREAK

Johnson's recording career was given a start by a record salesman. In the 1930's, record salesmen would load up the trunks of their cars with Blues records. Then the salesmen would travel to the rural areas and sell the records to the black people who lived there. One day, a record salesman heard Robert Johnson play and recommended him to his friend Don Law who had come South to record the rural artists for Vocalion Records.

In November of 1936 and June of 1937 Johnson did several recording sessions for Vocalion, now owned by Columbia Records. In those few sessions, Johnson cut 29 sides, and left a treasure chest of music to future generations. The records showcase Johnson's dazzling guitar and vocal style, and demonstrate the songwriting abilities that have made him a legend among legends. Muddy Waters claims Johnson as his main influence, and among those who have recorded Robert's songs are The Rolling Stones ("Love In Vain"), Cream ("Crossroads") and Taj Mahal ("Sweet Home Chicago").

When Johnson was brought to San Antonio, Texas to record for Law, he found trouble hours after he got to town. Law was called to bail Johnson out of jail, and found him with his clothes torn, his guitar broken and his face bloody.

MYSTERIOUS MURDER

Robert was a small, slender man who was extremely shy around other musicians. But his shyness left him when he was around beautiful women, and that proved to be his downfall. Some said that they were surprised Johnson lived as long as he did because he would go after women who caught his eye, not caring if she had a boyfriend or husband. Johnson's death remains as much a mystery as his life. Some stories say he was poisoned by a jealous girlfriend, some tell of him being stabbed to death by a jealous husband. Whatever the case Robert Johnson died in 1937, leaving the world to mourn his passing and celebrate his music.

Elvis Presley makes it "big" on "Big Boy" Crudups song, "That's All Right Mama."

BIG BOY CRUDUP — THE MAN WHO HELPED MAKE ELVIS

A big man indeed is Arthur "Big Boy" Crudup (pronounced "Crood-up"). Standing well over six feet tall with the muscular frame of a man who works hard, Big Boy is no stranger to the Blues. While Elvis Presley was making his fame and fortune in 1955 with the smash hit "That's All Right, Mama", the man that wrote the song — Big Boy Crudup — was driving a farm tractor in Mississippi.

Born in 1905, in Forest, Mississippi, Arthur was the son of a guitar playing farmhand. Crudup got the nickname of "Big Boy" as a youth not only because he was tall, but he looked even taller because he had a small head and almost no neck. Big Boy weighed almost 220 pounds when he came to Chicago in 1940 with a gospel group called "The Harmonizing Four." After Crudup broke from the group he "lived" in a wooden crate beneath the elevated train station at 39th Street, and sang for handouts on street corners.

Arthur "Big Boy" Crudup.

I'M MAKIN' EVERYBODY RICH

In 1941, Big Boy was discovered singing on a street corner by talent scout Lester Melrose. Soon Big Boy was recording at Bluebird Records, singing in his high-pitched voice in a style much like the hollers of the fieldhands that Big Boy heard in his youth.

Big Boy recorded for many different record labels from 1941 to 1954 using several names (Elmer James, Perry Lee Crudup). This was a common practice for Blues singers in the early days. Big Boy quit recording in 1954 because, he says, "I realized that I was making everybody rich, and here I was poor."

CHEATED OUT OF $60,000

Besides Elvis Presley, Big Boy Crudup's songs have been recorded by Elton John, Creedence Clearwater Revival, Rod Stewart and other big stars. Big Boy never received any money from any of these people because of the record companies' red tape. In 1971 Big Boy and his children drove all the way from Virginia to New York City to finally get $60,000 in long awaited royalities (money paid to a song writer when someone else records his song). As Big Boy sat in the office of Presley's song publishers waiting for the check that had been promised him, a lawyer told him the president of the company decided it would be cheaper to fight it out in court than to just hand over a check to Big Boy!

Big Boy says "I was born poor, I live poor and I'm going to die poor." Big Boy was right. On March 28, 1974, Big Boy died poor. He never saw any money from his song writing efforts. But as Big Bill Broonzy says, "When you hear Elvis, you're hearing Big Boy Crudup." And though he had no money, Big Boy was one of the true fathers of Rock-n-Roll.

MUDDY WATERS —
LIKE A ROLLOING STONE

Deep in the heart of the Mississippi Delta country, in April of 1915, a man was born who would influence a generation of rock musicians. As a child, McKinley Morganfield loved to play in the muddy waters of the nearby bayou. Soon his grandmother began calling him Muddy Waters. The name stuck and the young boy grew up to be a Blues legend.

Muddy Waters formed his first band in 1932, calling on his strongest influences in music, Robert Johnson and Son House, two other Bluesmen who had their roots in the red clay of the Deep South. In 1940, Muddy left Mississippi to hone his playing skills in a travelling tent show. After several years Muddy felt he was ready to break into the Blues scene in Chicago. Things were tough at first, with Muddy driving a truck by day and playing small clubs by night. But in 1947, Blues great Big Bill Broonzy helped Muddy get some records made on the Aristocrat Label.

AN ELECTRIFYING GUITAR

Muddy used the electric guitar as a power tool, carving songs out of the hardships he experienced as a young man. He drilled his audience with distortion and feedback, making them sit up and take notice of his powerful Delta Blues. Throughout the 50's, Waters was one of the most popular players in Chicago's competitive scene.

Even though Muddy was changing the "Delta Blues" to the "Chicago Blues" almost by himself, he was not selling many records. Waters had a

Muddy Waters.

small hit with "I'm Your Hootchie-Cootchie Man," but he never had a number one song on the charts. His soul stirring music with its distortion and feedback were not commonly used on records in the 50's and Muddy's music remained mostly unknown until a couple of young Englishmen heard Muddy in the early 60's. Those young men, John Lennon and Mick Jagger, were greatly influenced by Muddy Waters.

The Rolling Stones took their name from a Muddy Waters song, and when the Beatles first came to America, the two people they wanted to see were Bo Diddley and Muddy Waters. Soon, American teenagers were taking an interest in Blues music, and guitar players like Eric Clapton and Jimi Hendrix rode the wave of fame and fortune using the styles pioneered by that Delta Bluesmen, Muddy Waters. Today, every Rock-n-Roll guitar player from Eddie Van Halen to The Edge owes a debt to Muddy Waters.

B.B. KING — GUITAR SUPERSTAR

If anyone could be considered the "Superstar" of the Blues, it would be B.B. King. King and his guitar "Lucille" have been turning out hit after hit on the R & B charts since 1953. B.B. has toured the world and played for presidents and kings.

Riley B. King was born in the fall of 1925 in the Delta town of Itta Bena, Mississippi. Riley's family was a musical one. His grandfather played guitar and both his parents sang. King had a good voice and sang in the church choir. When his parents broke up and his mother died, King became a tenant farmer. Riley planted, hoed and picked cotton alone. And he was only nine years old.

B.B. PLAYS THE BLUES

When King wasn't working in the fields he was listening to records. Besides listening to Blues players like Blind Lemon Jefferson, King was listening to Jazz artists like Charlie Christianson and Django Reinhart. (Django was one of the fastest guitar players ever, and he only had two fingers on his left hand.)

King never really set out to have a career in show business, and didn't really play the blues until he was in his twenties. King's family thought the

B.B. King

Blues was "Devil's music," so B.B. spent most of his time singing gospel music. Now and then B.B. would sneak off during the weekends to earn extra money playing the Blues.

THE BLUES BOY

In 1946 B.B. moved to Memphis to live with his cousin Bukka White. Bukka was a well-known Bluesman, famous for his slide guitar playing. B.B. got a job at radio station WDIA in Memphis using the name "Beale Street Blues Boy." When he started peforming, Riley King became Blues Boy King. Blues Boy was later shorten to B.B.

B.B. started to compete in amateur nights at the Palace Theater on Beale Street. First Prize was one dollar, and if the audience didn't like someone's singing they would boo and throw things at the performer!

B.B.'s career took off in 1951 when he recorded "Three O'Clock Blues." The song went to number one on the R & B charts and launched one of the most successful careers in Blues history.

B.B.'s single note lead guitar style and gospel vocal combined with jazz chording make him unique among his generation of Bluesmen. King's roots are in Blues but he has changed and grown over the years. B.B. still thrills his audiences, urging them to sing along with him, then letting loose with some dynamite blues riffs, showing everyone that B.B. is indeed still the King.

RAY CHARLES — THE BLIND MAN BOOGIES

When Ray Charles was eighteen years old and living in Florida, he asked a friend to pick a city that was farthest away from where they were, but still in the United States. His friend picked Seattle, Washington. Ray took the bus there, alone, the next day. Ray entered a talent show his first night in town, sang "Driftin' Blues" and won the contest. This story is made remarkable by the fact that Ray Charles lost his eyesight at the age of seven.

RAY LOSES HIS SIGHT

Born September 23, 1930 in Albany, Georgia, Ray Charles Robinson's life and music have been an inspiration to millions of people. Ray's early life in

Ray Charles

Greensville, Florida had more than its share of tragedy. When Ray was four, his younger brother drowned in a washtub before Ray could call his mother for help. Ray started going blind when he was five, and was completely sightless by the age of seven. Doctors later said it was glaucoma that made him lose his sight, but Ray isn't so sure. He remembers being fascinated with the sun and staring into its blinding flames.

"You're blind not stupid. You lost your sight not your mind." Ray says those words spoken by his mother, Aretha, gave him the strength and courage he needed to become a successful musician and millionaire by the age of 30. Charles went to the St. Augustine School for the Deaf and Blind in Orlando, Florida where he learned to play classical piano works by Mozart and Chopin. But Ray still loved to play the boogie-woogie piano style that his neighbor Wylie Pittman taught him when he was a young boy.

Ray's mother died when he was fifteen and soon he made the trip to Seattle that would set him on the course to fame and fortune. Ray landed a job at a club called The Rockin' Chair, where he impressed people with his emotional singing and musical styles that included Jazz, Country, Gospel and Blues. Ray began making records that were inspirational to a whole new generation of musicians playing Rock-n-Roll and Soul music. In 1960 "Georgia On My Mind" became Ray's first number one hit, followed by "Hit the Road Jack" in 1961.

MICHAEL JACKSON'S BIGGEST INFLUENCE

Today, Ray is president of Ray Charles Enterprises in California, a company that has two recording studios, a rehearsal hall and offices for booking musicians. Ray recently played on "We Are The World." Charles also tours 300 days a year with a seventeen piece band. Ray does his own cooking, is an avid reader (he reads braille), can type seventy words a minute and plays a mean game of chess. Some of the biggest Rock-n-Roll stars, from Elton John to Michael Jackson, say Ray Charles was their biggest influence. About his blindness, Ray says, "There are many things you can see without the eye, 95 per cent of seeing isn't important anyway. I see as much through touch as most people do through seeing."

Ray Charles and his orchestra with the Raelets recording exclusively for ABC-Paramount.

Ray Charles has overcome personal tragedy and physical handicap to become one of the greatest and most influential musicians of the twentieth century.

HANK WILLIAMS — THE LONESOME COUNTRY SUPERSTAR

The young man looked out from the stage at the Grand Ole Opry in Nashville, Tennessee. It was his first appearance there, and he was nervous. The crowd didn't recognize him and their applause was half-hearted when his name was announced. Finally, Hank Williams closed his eyes, bent his knee and crooned into the microphone, "I got a feeling called the blues/ Since my baby said good-bye/ Lord, I don't know what I'm doin'/ All I do is sit and cry."

When Hank sang the word "blues" and yodeled that high note, the crowd suddenly recognized the latest hit song being played on the radio, "Lovesick Blues." The audience identified the hillbilly singer in the big cowboy hat as THE Hank Williams. That night, June 11, 1949 put Hank on the road to stardom. It was the first time ever that

Hank Williams performing on radio station WSM.

a singer making his first appearance at the Grand Ole Opry Was called back for six encores! Hank Williams went on to become a legend in his own time, crossing over from Country to Pop music. Since his self-destructive death in 1952, Williams songs have been recorded by hundreds of Country, Pop, Blues and Rock artists.

FROM DIRT POOR TO RISING STAR

For Hank Williams, that moment at the Grand Ole Opry could not have come soon enough. Born September 17, 1923 in Georgiana, Alabama, Hank's family was dirt poor, and his father was in and out of mental institutions as a result of shell shock received during World War I. When he was young, Hank learned to play guitar from an old black man named Rufe Payne. When Hank grew older, he auditioned for the Grand Ole Opry but was rejected. However, the Louisiana Hayride, another radio show that broadcast all over the South, liked Williams and hired him for their show.

Hank's rise to stardom was helped further by Fred Rose and his son Wesley. Fred Rose was the first music publisher in Nashville. In 1946, Hank Williams approached Fred and Westly while they were playing ping-pong. Since they were not busy at the time they agreed to listen to some songs Hank had written. After listening to half-dozen songs from the tall, skinny stranger with a "tear" in his voice, Fred Rose was still unsure of Hank's talent. He sent Williams off in the corner to write a song while he continued his game. Hank came back five minutes later and sang "Mansion on the Hill" and Rose immediately signed Hank to a contract. Fred Rose became Hank's manager, landing him a record contract with industry giant MGM. Soon Hank's name started turning up in the number one slot on Billboard magazine's Top Ten.

I'LL NEVER GET OUT OF THIS WORLD ALIVE

Rose helped Hank's career but he could not stop the self-destructive habits that killed Hank just three short years after his brilliant rise to stardom.

Hank's life was much like his songs. Williams was a lonely man whose childhood was tragic. Hank's marriage to Audret Williams was very unhappy and in his songs such as "Cold, Cold Heart" and "I'm So Lonesome I Could Cry," Williams touches on the sadness and bitterness of his own lost love. Hank was not alone with these types of problems and many of his records were bought by people who felt the same way.

THE BEGINNING OF THE END

By the fall of 1952, Hank's career lay in ruins. Williams had been fired by the Grand Ole Opry for drunkeness and divorced by his wife who demanded, and got, half his song writing royalties. To make matters worse, Williams was openly scorned by promoters who had to cancel shows when Hank showed up drunk or didn't show up at all. All these pressures put on Hank only increased his dependence on alcohol and pills.

Hank Williams, the Lonesome Superstar.

PAYING THE PRICE OF FAME

On New Years night, 1953, Hank was booked to play in Canton, Ohio. It was a long ride from Montgomery, Alabama, to Canton. A winter storm was raging. A young man named Charles Carr was hired by Hank to drive him to the concert.

The Cadillac never made it to Canton on that stormy night. Somewhere around Oak Hill, West Virginia, Carr tried to awaken his famous passenger. But he couldn't. Hank Williams was dead. Hank had died somewhere in Tennessee without saying a word. The official cause of death was heart attack brought on by excessive drinking. The barbituates Williams was taking also contributed to his death. The show went on in Canton that night, with people in the band and the audience weeping uncontrollably.

Ironically, Hank's last hit, "I'll Never Get Out of This World Alive," was a humorous song about life's little problems. After the singer's death, this song became a mammoth hit for MGM. Many of Hank's albums were rereleased to smashing sales.

Twenty-five thousand people turned out for Hank's funeral in Montgomery and several thousand were able to view the casket. Seven women fainted and one woman had to be led from the church because she was hysterical.

All in all, Hank Williams lived a tragic life that led to an equally tragic death at the age of 29. No one can say what would have been if he had lived. Hank was just starting to come to terms with his problems when he died. Hank Williams has continued to be a huge moneymaker for MGM and Acuff-Rose Publishing, and there are now thirty albums out by Hank. His songs have been recorded by everyone from Ray Charles to Linda Ronstadt, and his son, Hank Williams, Jr., has become a star in his own right. Hank was sometimes sad, but he sang many songs that helped people laugh at their problems. Hank Williams paid the price of fame, but his songs are still a source of joy to millions.

FINAL WORD

The people mentioned in this book are just some of the biggest stars who changed popular music. A trip to the "Blues" section of your local record store or library will reveal the names of hundreds of people involved in the early years of commercial music. In fact, most libraries have numerous records and books on Jazz, Country, Rock and Big Band music. By reading and listening to the people who made it happen you will have a greater understanding of what you hear on the radio and television every day. And who knows, maybe someday, somewhere, somebody will be writing about your life and talents in a book!

THE JUKEBOX PLAYS THE TUNE

The thirty year old inventor crouched over the strange machine in his lab. Although he was deaf in one ear, his good ear could hear well — even into the future! He rotated the crank and spoke into the horn of his new invention, "Mary had a little lamb/ Its fleece was white as snow."

Thomas Edison then reset the stylus to the beginning of the tin foil cylinder and rotated the hand crank again. He heard his own voice saying: "Mary had a little lamb . . ."

So begins the story of a machine that is as much a part of American culture as apple pie and Chevy's. After months of experimenting in his laboratory, Thomas Edison had finally made a machine to reproduce the human voice. By putting together a wheel, a screw that turned a cylinder covered with tin foil, a stylus to make scratches on the foil and a horn that echoed the sounds the stylus was making, Edison changed the world!

THE PHONOGRAPH IS BORN

Edison had invented his machine to be used in business. But it wasn't long before music recording became its main function. The tin cylinders were replaced with wax, but Edison's machine didn't find true success until twelve years later when an enterprising saloon keeper named Louis Glass attached four listening tubes and a coin slot to the phonograph. On November 23, 1889, in San Francisco, California, the "Nickel in the Slot" was born.

People fell in love with the "Nickelodeon" or "Jukebox" as it would be called in future years. Whatever the name, Louis Glass' machine was making over $200 a month. By 1890 coin operated phonographs were being found everywhere from train stations to restaurants. Soon musicians were playing music in the turn-of-the-century version of today's high-tech, digital recording studios. Things were quite different in 1890. Wax cylinders could only be produced one at a time, so each one had to be recorded separately. That means the musician recorded two minutes worth of music, a new cylinder was put in the recorder, and the musician played the song again and again and again for each recording.

By 1906, the "Gable Automatic Entertainer," a jukebox that played the new, mass produced, 10-inch, flat records became the new fad. People could look through a glass window and see the records dropping onto the turntable. No need for headphones. Now everyone in the room could hear the music blasting through a forty-inch horn!

By 1908, people stopped dropping their coins into the nickelodeons. Suddenly everyone could afford their own phonographs. The price of the phonograph plummeted from $200 (a lot of money when an average worker of the day took home $25 a month!) to about $7.50. Thousands of Americans were not listening to phonographs in their own homes. And the jukebox took its place next to the gumball machines and player pianos in the penny arcade. It wouldn't be until the "Roaring Twenties" that Louis Glass' invention would make a comeback.

Another scientific breakthrough put the jukebox back on the road to popularity. In 1925, Bell Laboratories developed electronic amplification using vacuum tubes. This invention revolutionized American life. Now musicians could record into a microphone and boost the volume with an amplifier. The quality of recorded music increased dramatically, and now it could be heard on an even newer device — the radio.

The "Roaring Twenties" were in full swing and the jukebox was regaining popularity as millions of Americans went to "speakeasies" to eat and drink. Jukeboxes took on new designs and each company tried to outdo the other with flashing lights, colored glass, and large selections of records.

By the 1950's, jukeboxes were in every ice cream parlor, tavern and restaurant. The 45 R.P.M. record had been introduced by RCA in 1949, and they were perfect for the jukebox. For many teenagers, the jukebox at the local ice cream parlor was the first place they heard Rock-n-Roll.

Nowadays the jukebox has moved into the '80's, playing CD's and albums. Gone are the nickel slots. Todays machines take dollar bills! Generations have danced to the jukeboxes, and many of the old machines that are left today are worth tens of thousands of dollars. But the jukebox's impact on American culture remains immeasurable, as they helped bring music to an entire nation.